This book
belongs to:

Would you go to the city, be friends
fountain in it, travel by rickshaw, eat l
and a deer-stalker hat, keep a pet touc
for fun and sleep in a bunk bed? Or wo
ghost, live in a wigwam with a trampoli
and mash, wear a denim jacket with a t
fashion model, blow bubbles and sl
the seaside, be friends with a Viking, liv
in it, travel by limousine, eat a box of ch
hat and fluffy mules, keep a pet elephar
and sleep in a kennel? Or would you go
in a tower block with a secret door in it, t
a poncho with stilettos and a furry ho
line dancing and sleep on a camp bed? O
be friends with an alien, live in a ligh
canoe, eat a bag of crisps, wear a kilt w
a pet unicorn, be an astronaut, do

ith a pirate, live in a spaceship with a
ster, wear a suit of armour with trainers
n, be a deep-sea diver, build a snowman
ld you go to the moon, be friends with a
in it, travel by paddle boat, eat sausages
ra and wedges, keep a pet monkey, be a
ep in a shoe? Or would you go to
in a fairy palace with a ping pong table
colates, wear a grass skirt with a cowboy
, be a hairdresser, go on a bouncy castle
to a desert, be friends with a knight, live
avel by helicopter, eat a hamburger, wear
, keep a pet spider, be a magician, go
r would you go to the top of a mountain,
house with chandeliers in it, travel by
ith winkle pickers and a sombrero, keep
a jigsaw and sleep in a hammock?

In memory of Henry Brown

N.S.

To everyone at Browsers Bookshop

P.G.

PUFFIN BOOKS

UK | USA | Canada | Ireland | Australia
India | New Zealand | South Africa

Puffin Books is part of the Penguin Random House group of companies
whose addresses can be found at global.penguinrandomhouse.com.

www.penguin.co.uk www.puffin.co.uk www.ladybird.co.uk

First published by Doubleday 2003
Picture Corgi edition published 2004
First published by Puffin 2018
This edition published 2023

009

Printed in China

The authorized representative in the EEA is Penguin Random House Ireland,
Morrison Chambers, 32 Nassau Street, Dublin D02 YH68

A CIP catalogue record for this book is available from the British Library

ISBN: 978–0–141–37931–9

All correspondence to:
Puffin Books, Penguin Random House Children's,
One Embassy Gardens, 8 Viaduct Gardens, London SW11 7BW

YOU
CHOOSE
Imagine you could have anything you wanted!
What sort of things do you mean?
Just turn the pages of this book, have a look and choose.
Nick Sharratt & Pippa Goodhart
PUFFIN

If you could go anywhere,

where would you go?

Who would you like for

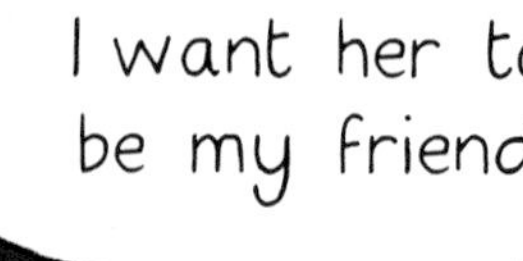
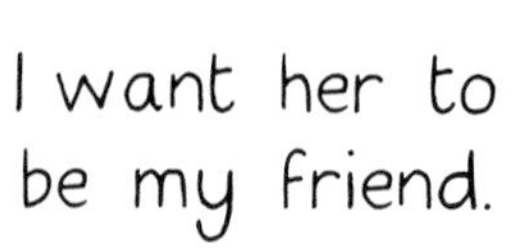

family and friends?

What kind of home

would you choose?

And what would you put in it?

This is my chair.
A secret door. What could be on the other side?
WELCOME

Would you travel with wheels or wings?

Or perhaps choose one of these other things?

When you got hungry,
What should I start with?

what would you eat?
Jelly and ice cream!
And pancakes!

What would you wear?

Nothing at all!

Choose some shoes ...

... and perhaps a hat?

Why not get yourself a pet...

or two or three or more?

Is there a job

you'd like to do?

What would you do...

...for fun?

And when you got tired
and felt like a snooze,

where would you sleep? You choose. Goodnight!

Would you go to the desert, be frien
caravan with a drum set in it, travel by a
with flip-flops and a furry hat, keep a p
for fun and sleep in a cradle? Or would y
live in a cave with a swimming pool in
wear a tuxedo with Roman sandals and a
go on a roller coaster and sleep in
outer space, be friends with a baby,
on it, travel by steam train, eat a water
and lacy boots, keep a pet polar bear,
sleep in a hammock? Or would you go
live in a cottage with a secret door in it,
wear a bikini with clogs and a top
bird-watching and sleep on a nest? Or
be friends with a vampire, live in a tree
by space shuttle, eat squid, wear a bow
keep a pet bat, be a deep-sea diver,

ds with Superwoman, live in a bright
ship, eat sponge cake, wear a feather boa
t dragon, be a clown, make phone calls
u go to the seaside, be friends with a wolf,
, travel by helicopter, drink milkshakes,
onnet, keep a pet lizard, be an astronaut,
bed of flowers? Or would you go to
ive on a toadstool with a glitter light
elon, wear dungarees with a sailor's hat
e an architect, go bungee jumping and
o the moon, be friends with a gangster,
ravel by paraglider, eat corn-on-the-cob,
at, keep a pet panda, be a pilot, go
would you go to the top of a waterfall,
house with a rocking horse in it, travel
tie with ballet shoes and a panama hat,
ead a book and sleep in a space bed?

YOU CHOOSE IN SPACE
Nick Sharratt Pippa Goodhart
A NEW STORY EVERY TIME – what will YOU CHOOSE?
YOU CHOOSE YOUR DREAMS
Nick Sharratt Pippa Goodhart
A NEW STORY EVERY TIME – what will YOU CHOOSE?
YOU CHOOSE FAIRY TALES
Nick Sharratt Pippa Goodhart
A NEW STORY EVERY TIME – what will YOU CHOOSE?
Giles Andreae Nick Sharratt
Pants
Animal Pants
Giles Andreae Nick Sharratt
Party Pants
20 FIN-TASTIC YEARS!
Shark in the Park!
Over 300,000 snapped up!
A fin-tastic sequel to Shark in the Park!
Shark in the Dark!
Nick Sharratt
Nick Sharratt
Shark in the Park on a Windy Day!
Oh No! Shark in the Snow!
FIN-TASTIC FESTIVE FUN!
Nick Sharratt
DAISY Eat Your Peas
from the author of Oi FROG!
Kes Gray Nick Sharratt
DAISY Yuk!
Kes Gray Nick Sharratt
DAISY Really, Really
Kes Gray Nick Sharratt
DAISY Tiger Ways
Kes Gray Nick Sharratt
DAISY 006 and a Bit
Nick Sharratt
DAISY You Do!
Kes Gray Nick Sharratt
Why not choose
some more books
illustrated by Nick Sharratt?